This book
belongs to

_____

_____

For John,
for his unwavering support and
patience beyond the call of duty,
with all my love
Lynne

First published in 2004 in Great Britain by Gullane Children's Books
This paperback edition published in 2005 by
GULLANE CHILDREN'S BOOKS
an imprint of Pinwheel Limited
Winchester House, 259-269 Old Marylebone Road, London NW1 5XJ

1 3 5 7 9 10 8 6 4 2

Text and illustrations © Lynne Chapman 2004

ISBN 1-86233-383-1 hardback
ISBN 1-86233-480-3 paperback

Printed and bound in China

When You're Not Looking!

Lynne
Chapman

GULLANE
CHILDREN'S BOOKS

Things aren't always
        what they seem.
This may look like
        a normal scene.

BUT these creatures
    are a crazy crew –
You won't believe
        what they all do

...**when
    you're not
        looking!**

Rhinos love to wallow, In squelchy muddy hollows.

But they sometimes use the trees As a flying trapeze

...when you're not Looking!

Everyone knows,
Bats
hang from
their toes.

But no-one
ever lets on
They wear
a fez or stetson

...**when
you're not
looking!**

People say that
pigs
are chubby,
Greedy too,
and also grubby.

BUT they really
are quite chic,
Setting fashions
every week

...when
you're not
Looking!

Worms are good at wriggling,
They're not so good at giggling.

But if they put their false teeth in,
They can flash a cheeky grin

...**when you're not Looking!**

Gerbils play
for hours on end,
By themselves
or with a friend.

But what
they really
love the most
Is eating
marmalade on toast

**...when
you're not
Looking!**

If **COWS** aren't
busy chewing,
They'll most probably
be mooing.

BUT though there
is no proof, they
Can rustle up
a soufflé

...**when
you're not
looking!**

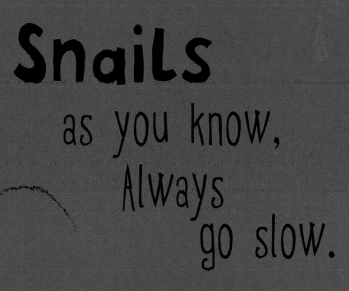

Snails as you know,
Always
go slow.

But they
love to change
the pace
With a
turbo-powered race

...when
you're not
Looking!

Contented **chickens** peck the ground
And make a happy
          clucking sound.

But they love
blasting into space,
From their hen-house
          rocket base

...**when
you're not
Looking!**

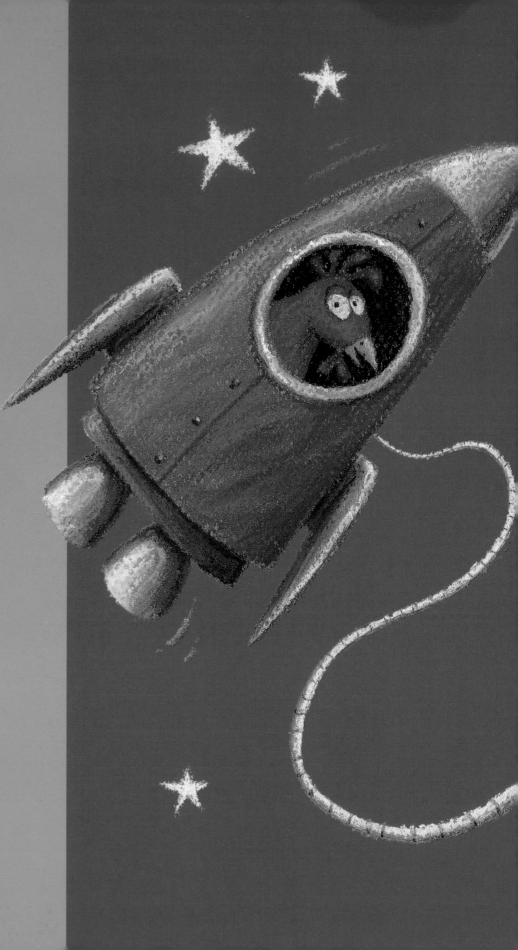

So now you know...

cheerio!

Other Gullane Children's Books
for you to enjoy

Also illustrated by
Lynne Chapman

Big Bad Wolf IS Good

Simon Puttock ● Lynne Chapman

Little Giant

Simone Lia

My Dad!

Charles Fuge

Snog the Frog

Tony Bonning ● Rosalind Beardshaw